STRONG, HEALTHY GIRLS

NUTRITION AND EXERCISE

By Emma Huddleston

CONTENT CONSULTANT

Jenny Oliphant, EdD, MPH
Community Outreach Coordinator and Research Associate
Healthy Youth Development-Prevention Research Center
University of Minnesota
School of Medicine, Division of General Pediatrics and Adolescent Health

Essential Library

An Imprint of Abdo Publishing | abdobooks.com

abdobooks.com

Published by Abdo Publishing, a division of ABDO, PO Box 398166, Minneapolis, Minnesota 55439.

Printed in the United States of America, North Mankato, Minnesota.
082020
012021

Cover Photo: Laboo Studio/Shutterstock Images
Interior Photos: iStockphoto, 8, 10–11, 22, 25, 35, 36–37, 40, 45, 48–49, 56–57, 59, 62, 64–65, 72, 75, 84–85, 96; London Eye/iStockphoto, 12; Film Studio/iStockphoto, 14; Fang Xia Nuo/iStockphoto, 18; Light Field Studios/Shutterstock Images, 20–21; Media Production/iStockphoto, 28; Bernard Bobo/iStockphoto, 31; Praetorian Photo/iStockphoto, 32–33; Monkey Business Images/iStockphoto, 42–43, 92; Dragon Images/iStockphoto, 47; Carlos Gaw/iStockphoto, 52; Juan Monino/iStockphoto, 54–55, 89; Lara Belova/iStockphoto, 66; Wave Break Media/iStockphoto, 68–69; Shutterstock Images, 76, 78–79; Pollyana Ventura/iStockphoto, 82; Marcos Calvo/iStockphoto, 86; Raw Pixel/iStockphoto, 94–95; Rich Vintage/iStockphoto, 98–99

Editor: Melissa York
Series Designer: Nikki Nordby

Library of Congress Control Number: 2019954387
Publisher's Cataloging-in-Publication Data

Names: Huddleston, Emma, author.
Title: Nutrition and exercise / by Emma Huddleston
Description: Minneapolis, Minnesota : Abdo Publishing, 2021 | Series: Strong, healthy girls | Includes online resources and index.
Identifiers: ISBN 9781532192210 (lib. bdg.) | ISBN 9781098210113 (ebook)
Subjects: LCSH: Teenage girls--Nutrition--Juvenile literature. | Physical fitness for girls--Juvenile literature. | Exercise for girls--Juvenile literature. | Body image in girls--Juvenile literature. | Wellness--Juvenile literature.
Classification: DDC 155.533--dc23

CONTENTS

MEET DR. JENNY 4

TAKE IT FROM ME 6

CHAPTER ONE
TOO MUCH FAST FOOD 8

CHAPTER TWO
TRICKY FOOD LABELS 18

CHAPTER THREE
ALWAYS AT THE GYM 28

CHAPTER FOUR
HOW DO I LOOK? 40

CHAPTER FIVE
HIDDEN SUGAR 52

CHAPTER SIX
MAKING TIME FOR MOVING 62

CHAPTER SEVEN
THE FAD DIET 72

CHAPTER EIGHT
GOT CAFFEINE? 82

CHAPTER NINE
TRAINING FOR TRYOUTS 92

A SECOND LOOK 102
PAY IT FORWARD 104
GLOSSARY 106
ADDITIONAL RESOURCES 108
INDEX 110
ABOUT THE AUTHOR 112

DR. JENNY

Jenny Oliphant believes all young people deserve to thrive, not just survive. Her work focuses on making sure parents, professionals, and young people themselves have the information, skills, and tools to make that happen. She's an expert in adolescent sexual health, youth development, health education, and sports education.

Dr. Jenny holds a master's of public health in community health education from the University of Minnesota and a doctorate from the University of Saint Thomas in educational leadership. She speaks locally and nationally about youth development, peer education, and pregnancy prevention. Her background includes experiences as a health educator and adjunct instructor in health for community health educators, health teachers, and epidemiologists in training.

Dr. Jenny is the community outreach coordinator and research associate for the Healthy Youth Development-Prevention Research Center at the University of Minnesota in the School of Medicine, Division of General Pediatrics and Adolescent Health. There, she helps families and health providers design and implement youth-friendly health programming supported by current research. At Walden University, as a contributing faculty member, she teaches students the art and science of becoming community-engaged public health professionals working for social change.

Dr. Jenny teaches future pediatricians and nurses how to interview teens about their sexual health. She recently wrapped up a five-year study in which she worked with middle schools to develop teaching plans to improve students' social and emotional health. Her newest research is focused on helping clinics better engage with adolescent patients. She's also working on training dentists and hygienists to recommend the human papillomavirus vaccine to parents and young people.

Dr. Jenny has worked as a consultant for a series of books written for teens and focused on topics in adolescent health. She's also served as a federal accuracy reviewer for numerous curricula used in programming funded by the US government's Office of Adolescent Health.

She lives in Minneapolis, Minnesota, with her teen children, her husband, and her bulldog, Sid. In the future, she dreams of living and working in Berlin, Germany, and continues to practice her German, in hopes of making her dream come true.

TAKE IT FROM ME

Nutrition is part of daily life. That's obvious, considering you have to think about what you want to eat multiple times a day. Still, many girls are figuring out what eating habits are healthy for them. As their bodies change from childhood into adolescence, their nutritional needs change. Between the pressures of school, family, and other activities, it can be hard to find food that's fast, affordable, tasty, and also healthy. Some girls eat fast food or drink coffee. Others might try following a diet. Exercise is also an important part of keeping healthy. Lots of girls don't want to be active after a long day at school or work. Some are nervous to try new activities. Others overwork their bodies because they don't know when to stop.

Balancing nutrition and exercise is challenging for girls and women of all ages. Learning to make meals and buy healthy foods are skills people develop over time. A girl's exercise needs change as her body grows.

The way I see it, exercise and nutrition go hand in hand. If I change one routine, it affects the other. For example, when I was running every day during track season, my appetite increased.

I needed more food to have the energy to get through training. After the season, my nutrition and exercise habits changed again. I didn't work out as much, so I didn't need as much food. If I ate a big meal, I felt so full that I was uncomfortable. I had to adjust my habits to find a healthy balance.

While you form nutrition and exercise habits, remember that you are not alone. Friends and family members also have to balance nutrition and exercise. Consider talking with them about what they do and why. You might get new ideas, or you might learn a lesson about a habit gone wrong. Sometimes, just admitting you have a question is the hardest part. Don't be afraid to ask your doctor or someone you trust for help. I can guarantee that someone else has wondered the same thing before.

You need exercise and nutritious food to be healthy and live your best life. You can create healthy habits in countless ways. The key point to remember is to do what's best for you, no matter what other people are doing.

XOXO,
EMMA

DRIVE
THRU

CHAPTER ONE

TOO MUCH FAST FOOD

Bright signs for fast-food restaurants might seem to be everywhere. Some light up. Others have advertisements and deals written in big letters. It can be easy and fun to stop at drive-throughs. Often, fast-food menus even have tempting treats or specials at certain times of the day to entice people to stop.

It's common for girls and people of all ages to give in to fast-food temptations. In 2019, more than one-third of US children and teens ate fast food daily. The meals may have been convenient. But these foods can have negative effects on a person's health. Fast food is often high in sodium and saturated fats. These fats are solid at room temperature. Fast food often leads to weight gain. Eating too much of it can also lead to heart disease or diabetes.

Health experts agree that it's very difficult to stick to healthy foods when eating out. Many traditional restaurant meals are also low in nutrients and high in fat, sugar, and calories.

Unfortunately, it's easy to form a fast-food habit that's bad for the body in the long run.

SAM'S STORY

"Sam, don't forget to pack a lunch!" Sam's mom yelled upstairs to her.

Sam burst into the kitchen, zipping her jacket on the run.

"Mom, I'm almost late for work. I don't have time to make anything," Sam said. She grabbed her car keys off the counter. "I'll just pick up some food on the way."

"Didn't you do that yesterday?" her mom asked. She put her hands on her hips and looked at Sam.

"Yeah, but I don't mind. It's easier. Bye!" Sam called, closing the door behind her.

Sam had turned 16 at the end of the school year that May. She enjoyed the freedom that came with being old enough to drive. She could easily visit friends and get to her job at the movie theater. The theater was located near several fast-food restaurants, grocery stores, and small shops.

***

Sam hit three red lights in a row. She sighed. She wouldn't

TALK ABOUT IT

- **How often do you eat out at fast-food spots or other restaurants?**
- **Do you think you eat out too much? Why or why not? How do you know how much is too much?**

have time to stop for food after all. *Maybe I should go to the fast-food place next door on my break.*

"Good afternoon, Sam," her coworker Gabby said as Sam finally walked in.

"Hey, Gabby," Sam said. "Did you make plans for lunch already? I'm going next door on my break if you want to come too."

"Sure! I want that new burger that just came out. It looked great on YouTube."

"Yeah, it looks fantastic," Sam agreed.

Sam enjoyed working with Gabby. They both enjoyed treating themselves to fast food on their breaks and ate next door frequently. Sam was making more money this summer than she had the previous summer. Now that she could drive, she could take extra work shifts. To Sam, spending five or ten dollars eating out each day was worth it.

***

On one of the last days of summer, Sam was getting dressed for work and noticed her shirt was tight. The buttons pressed gently against her skin. *I must have put on some weight*, Sam thought. She felt self-conscious and a bit upset with herself for eating out so much. She went downstairs.

TALK ABOUT IT

- **What are some main reasons you or others may choose to eat fast food?**
- **How might fast-food advertisements affect people's decisions? What ideas do fast-food restaurants put in their messages to help sell their products? Do you trust or believe the restaurants?**
- **Sam thinks about her fast-food habits one day at a time. How might thinking about her fast-food habits over the long term change her perspective?**

To Sam, spending five or ten dollars eating out each day was worth it.

“Mom, have you noticed that I’ve gained weight this summer?”

“What makes you think that?” Her mom stopped what she was doing to look at Sam.

“Well, my shirt has been feeling tight, and I’ve been eating out a lot at work.”

“Sam,” her mom said gently, “it’s true that eating fast food can be unhealthy, but instead of being worried about how you look, focus on how you feel. You need nutrients! They'll help your body feel back to normal. If you want to eat better foods, try packing a lunch. I just went to the store."

> "Instead of being worried about how you look, focus on how you feel."

"Thanks, Mom," Sam said.

Sam packed a lunch during the first week of school. She included a few snacks, too, in case she got hungry. Soon, her new habit felt normal.

***

"Hey, Sam, want to go grab food next door?" Gabby asked as the girls' break began one day at work.

"Actually, I was thinking of walking to the grocery store instead. I want to get an apple and some cheese and crackers," she said.

"Oh, yeah, I forgot there was one across the street. I'll come too," Gabby said, and the girls walked together to get food.

TALK ABOUT IT

- **What do you think is the main reason people should limit how much fast food they eat? What are some other reasons?**
- **If you could change a part of the fast-food industry, what would you change and why?**
- **Which part of the advice from Sam's mom do you think is most important? Why?**
- **How is Sam's new habit at work healthier than before?**

ASK THE EXPERT

Sam realized fast food was changing her body and decided to change her habits. Choosing to walk to a grocery store not only gives her exercise but also opens up more healthy food options.

Many fast-food meals and packaged foods contain saturated and trans fat and added salt and sugar. Those ingredients are unhealthy and can lead to many health issues. Saturated and trans fats should only make up 7 to 10 percent of a person's daily calories. However, many popular food items contain surprisingly high amounts. For example, two slices of bacon contain as much saturated fat as an adult should consume in one day. Such foods are not bad to eat on a limited basis, but they can cause problems if eaten regularly.

The National Center for Health Statistics found that 17 percent of children and teens in the United States were obese in 2019. The researchers linked weight gain to eating fast food.

If you find yourself eating fast food often, you can still make healthy choices. Choosing grilled food instead of fried and putting sauces on the side are ways to limit calories. Additionally, getting smaller portions is often a healthier option than combo or value packs.

GET **HEALTHY**

- If you pack your lunch or often make other meals for yourself, plan what you will eat in advance and make a grocery list. These simple actions save money in the long run and make shopping easy for you and your family.
- Skip eating packaged foods. Spend your money on cheaper, healthier, and fresher foods instead.
- Avoid saturated fats and trans fat. They are often in foods such as butter, fatty meats, fried food, and baked goods. Those types of fat can lead to heart disease, diabetes, or other health issues down the road.

THE LAST WORD FROM **EMMA**

The main way I keep myself out of fast-food lines is packing a lunch. At first, I thought packed lunches would be drab and inconvenient. But I discovered the opposite. Packed lunches are quick, easy, and delicious. After all, I choose what to put in them! Sometimes I make a sandwich or salad based on something that looked tasty in a restaurant advertisement. I look for the same ingredients at the store and make it myself. Not only is it healthier, but it's also cheaper. Plus, I can add any side dishes I want to my meal, like fruit or trail mix. I know that if I tried to get that much food eating out, it would cost me much more. And I would have to waste time and gas money driving to a restaurant. Now I just need to grab my lunchbox.

CHAPTER TWO

TRICKY FOOD LABELS

When you look down a store aisle, words and colors may seem to be jumping off the shelves at you. A can of cherry soda has the word *antioxidant* on it. A bag of chips has the words *all natural* in large print. A can of noodle soup is labeled *whole grain*. Many people think these words are there to help them find healthier food options. But it's smart to question how healthy packaged food can really be.

Is it possible that all food has some health benefit? Well, that's what food marketing wants you to think. Selling food is a business, and professional marketing teams work hard to attract buyers. Some big companies spend up to 15 percent of their budgets on marketing. They spend more money on ways to get consumers to buy their products than on finding ways to make foods healthier. Health trends such as eating gluten-free or organic foods have risen in the past ten years. So marketing experts often emphasize healthy aspects to their foods and downplay the unhealthy parts. For example, fruit smoothies may be marketed as low sodium, but the advertisements fail to point out the high levels of sugar in most of these drinks.

Food marketing can be misleading.

Food marketing can be misleading. Luckily, you can cut through tricky advertisements by paying attention to nutrition facts.

TARA'S STORY

Riiiiing! Lunchtime. Tara popped open her purple lunchbox and took out a homemade wrap. She also had a banana and a gluten-free granola bar.

Tara had used a purple lunchbox since she was a young girl. She remembered her dad packing her lunches. He often gave her sticks of vegetables and a sandwich. Now that she was older, Tara packed her own lunch and helped do the grocery shopping too. She often chose whole-grain crackers and gluten-free granola bars as healthy snacks.

"Those are my favorite granola bars," said her friend Carla, who was sitting nearby. "Are you gluten-free?" she asked.

"No, I just try to eat healthy foods," said Tara, shrugging.

"Ah, I see. Gluten is in lots of stuff," Carla said, nodding. "I'm allergic to wheat, so I also look for gluten-free food."

"I just figure that gluten-free is healthier because people talk about it so much." Tara unwrapped her granola bar and took a bite.

"Yeah, my mom always talks about how there's so many more options for gluten-free food now than when she was young," Carla said.

"It seems like lots of big brands have gluten-free stuff now," Tara said. She peeled her banana. As the girls ate, they talked about their favorite brands of yogurt and chips. Then the bell rang again, and Tara went to class.

TALK ABOUT IT

- **What types of foods do you eat most often? Is there a reason you eat certain foods more than others?**
- **When you think of healthy eating, what types of foods come to mind?**
- **How can food labels be helpful when people are making decisions about what to buy?**

***

The next time Tara went grocery shopping with her dad, she picked out a few of her favorite brands. She picked cereal labeled *no added sugar* and bread labeled *whole grain*. She let food labels help her decide which options were the healthiest. But when she walked through the candy aisle, she saw a bag of candy labeled *all natural*. She stopped walking. *All natural?* Tara usually considered all

She let food labels help her decide which options were the healthiest.

natural foods to be healthy. "But how can a sugary candy be healthy?" she wondered out loud.

When Tara got home, she looked up the meaning of *all natural* on the internet. She learned that the label can be misleading. Not everything in a food with that label was natural. It also wasn't an automatic sign of the food's nutritious value. Tara also came across several newspaper articles related to food marketing. After a few minutes of reading, she realized many food companies used misleading labels to get people to buy seemingly healthier products.

TALK ABOUT IT

- **What marketing terms besides *all natural* do you commonly see on food labels? Do you know what each term means?**
- **Like Tara, have you ever questioned food marketing? If yes, what did you want to learn more about? If no, why do you think you've trusted food labels?**

***

The next morning, Tara saw Carla in the school parking lot. They walked into school as Tara told Carla about what she learned.

Carla nodded. "Yup, marketing words on the front are often used to catch

TALK ABOUT IT

- **What is one way you can become more informed about the food you eat?**
- **Where can you look up reliable information about food labels and nutrition facts? Who can you talk to if you have questions about what to eat?**

your eye. I learned to rely on the nutrition label on the back because of my allergy."

"But lots of those ingredient lists are long and hard to read," Tara said.

"Well, some labels on the front are OK," said Carla. "Things like *gluten-free* are legal terms and have to be truthful. But others like *natural* don't mean much."

"I wish this were easier!" said Tara. "I guess I'll keep looking things up."

ASK THE EXPERT

Tara learned about misleading food marketing when she stopped to think about the product behind the label. She used common sense to separate a word on a label from the true nutrition of the food.

Food marketers know how to take advantage of people's desire to be healthy. They print buzzwords such as *natural* and *low fat* on packaged foods to make them seem healthier. Consumers often buy these products without realizing they are falling for clever marketing words. In fact, a study at the University of Houston tested how people view and rate the healthfulness of packaged foods. They showed people two images of the same product. One label had a marketing buzzword, and the other did not. People consistently rated the label with the buzzword as the healthier product.

By being aware of the business of marketing, you can outsmart tricky advertising. Reading nutrition facts and questioning seemingly healthy labels can help you choose healthy foods from crowded store shelves.

GET HEALTHY

- When in doubt, choose fresh foods over packaged or processed ones.
- Pay attention to the food label on the back of the product more than the label on the front. Read the first three ingredients—they make up most of the food.
- Ignore marketing that says *natural* and *no added sugars*. Those terms have loose definitions, so companies can put them on nearly any product.
- Use common sense when determining the healthfulness of a food. Ask yourself where the food came from. Does it grow naturally on Earth, or was it made in a factory?

THE LAST WORD FROM EMMA

It may seem obvious that a bag of frozen strawberries should only have one ingredient: strawberries. But I've found that it's necessary to check food labels for every food I buy.

When I took a nutrition class in high school, I expected it to be mainly about foods and which ones were healthiest. I was surprised to learn about the businesses behind food. My teacher pointed out how food marketing targets shoppers. Companies know people want to buy healthy foods, so they use labels to grab buyers' attention. But their goal is often centered on making money rather than providing the healthiest product. In that class, we learned how to spot misleading marketing so we'd fall for fewer tricky food labels.

1.5KG
1.5KG

CHAPTER THREE

ALWAYS AT THE GYM

How often do you think about exercise? Cars fill the parking lots at gyms. Social media posts show people working out in tight clothes or flexing their muscles. On one hand, getting a reminder to exercise can be helpful. We can all encourage each other to stay active. On the other hand, seeing other people taking workouts to the extreme can make many girls feel as though they are never fit enough. Too much pressure or unrealistic exercise routines can cause some girls to exercise—or think about exercising—constantly.

One million people in the United States struggle with exercise addiction. Many feel anxious when they miss a workout. Compulsive exercise can lead to mental and physical issues. Studies have found that extreme endurance training can lead to heart damage. People may develop an eating disorder or unhealthy body image. Women face additional risks when they exercise too much. They may experience bone loss or stop their menstrual cycle. These issues can overlap and cause more

The right amount of exercise is different for everyone.

stress or increase the urge to exercise.

Compulsive exercise can also hurt a girl's relationships with her friends or family. She may miss out on fun or even lose friends if she's always choosing the gym over other social activities. The right amount of exercise is different for everyone. By listening to your body and doing activities you enjoy, you can create a healthy routine.

MIKAYLA'S STORY

Beep! Beep! Beep! Beep! Mikayla smacked her alarm clock. She climbed out of bed and changed into workout clothes.

"Good morning, Mikayla," her dad said as she walked past.

"Hi, Dad. Bye, Dad," she said with a smile.

Typically, Mikayla arrived at school early three days a week to lift weights before class. Her footsteps echoed in the quiet gym. The weights made a *thud* as they hit the ground. Eventually, the sun brightened the windows in the room. Mikayla did a few more reps and then stopped her workout.

Mikayla changed into her school clothes. Her pants stretched over her calf muscles, and her strong shoulders easily carried

her backpack. Mikayla liked to keep her body in shape. She constantly thought about when she would have time to fit in her next workout.

***

When Mikayla got home, her dad was making dinner.

"So, what did you do for a workout today?" he asked.

"Lifted weights before school and swam after," Mikayla said. She set the table with two plates.

TALK ABOUT IT

- **How active are you during a typical week? Do you choose certain exercises to do? Why or why not?**
- **How can regular exercise benefit people?**

"Tough swimming workout?"

"Well, my arms felt sore after being in the water for a bit, but I pushed through," she said. Her dad chuckled.

"How long were you in the pool?"

"Nearly an hour," Mikayla responded.

"Whew! I think you are harder on yourself than any coach would be!" her dad said. "Just make sure you're taking care of yourself."

"Just make sure you're taking care of yourself."

"You know I do, Dad. I stretch every day."

***

Over the weekend, Mikayla ran several miles both days. On Sunday, she was sore and didn't look forward to the second round of running, but her mind was determined. *No pain, no gain,* she told herself.

After her run, she took a shower and put on a sweatshirt. She was chilly, even though the sun was shining bright. That night, she coughed several times, but she didn't notice until her dad mentioned it.

"Are you feeling all right?" her dad asked. "Sounds like you have a cough."

"Yeah, but I'm feeling fine."

"OK, but let me know if it gets worse tomorrow," he said.

Despite sleeping through her alarm, Mikayla felt tired the next day. She sat up and noticed she had a headache. Her cough was worse than yesterday too. *Ugh, I think I've got a cold*, she thought. *Maybe if I get my body moving, I can sweat it out. I still have time to get to the gym before school.*

"Hey, Mikayla, how are you feeling?" her dad asked.

"Fine," she said, then coughed loudly.

"You don't sound so good. Are you sure going to school early is a good idea? You don't want to wear your body down," he said. "Rest might be what you need."

"We'll see how I feel after," Mikayla said, and she hurried to get ready.

***

During the week, Mikayla's cold got worse. Her throat felt scratchy and her eyes were watery, but nothing stopped her from working out. She felt like her cold was lasting forever. Days and days had gone by, and she wasn't better. In fact, she felt more tired.

TALK ABOUT IT

- **Do you often push yourself doing physical activities? If yes, how do you feel when you work really hard? If no, what stops you?**
- **Mikayla's exercise habits seem to lack recovery time. Why is rest important?**

"Why don't you sleep in tomorrow?" Mikayla's dad suggested Friday night. "I'll make us eggs for breakfast. Extra sleep may help you fight that cold."

"Stop lecturing me about sleep, Dad," Mikayla snapped at him. He had mentioned getting extra sleep almost every night since she had gotten sick.

"Whoa, kiddo," he said. "Don't bite my head off. I'm just worried you aren't getting enough rest. You need to let your body recover."

"Yeah, I know, but you don't need to worry about me."

Mikayla walked to her room, sat down hard on her bed, and crossed her arms. Then she let herself relax. *I'm worried about myself,* she thought. She felt out of shape because she wasn't able to work out as much as usual. Additionally, she was behind on her homework. She almost fell asleep in class that afternoon, and she missed part of the lesson. *If only I could strengthen my body more, then my mind would be focused again.* Mikayla set her alarm and went to bed.

I'm worried about myself, she thought.

TALK ABOUT IT

- **Mikayla connects the strength of her body to the health of her mind. Do you think the state of your body or mind affects the other? Why or why not?**
- **Have you ever used working out as a solution to another health problem? What did you do? Did working out fix the issue or make it worse?**
- **How do you balance exercise with rest?**

ASK THE EXPERT

Mikayla wanted to always be at the top of her game. She didn't realize how important rest was to being her best. Her body was using energy in workouts and didn't have extra energy to fight off her illness. With more rest, Mikayla's cold might have healed faster. Instead, it got worse. Her lack of rest and nagging cold affected her body and mind.

Compulsive exercise easily leads to exhaustion. Exhaustion can have negative effects on all parts of life. One problem can quickly create others. For example, stress hormones such as adrenaline and cortisol in your body can weaken your immune system, which increases your chances of becoming sick or injured. Stress also can make it harder to sleep, and too much exercise can take time away from sleeping. That lack of sleep can affect your mood. People who exercise compulsively may become irritable or unfocused in school.

Exercise shapes and tests muscles, while rest lets them heal and become thicker and stronger. A healthy exercise routine includes both working out and recovery time. Compulsive exercise behavior can be managed in many ways. Some girls see a therapist. They talk about healthy mind-sets such as body image.

GET HEALTHY

- Do activities you enjoy. If you rarely enjoy your exercise, it could be a sign of compulsive exercise. A healthy exercise routine shouldn't feel like a chore.
- Switch up your routine. Doing a variety of different activities protects parts of your body from wearing out and lets you recover mentally and physically from tough workouts.
- Listen to your body. Feeling sore is normal after a tough workout, but you shouldn't always be sore. Soreness is a sign that your body hasn't recovered. It may need nutrients or rest to heal.
- Talk to a trusted adult, school counselor, or health care professional if you think you have an exercise addiction.

THE LAST WORD FROM EMMA

I once had a friend who exercised too much. She often pushed herself and aimed to never miss a workout because she wanted to look perfect. She organized her life around exercise instead of the other way around. Eventually, our friendship faded because she wouldn't make time to see me. Overall, a healthy exercise routine makes a girl feel good in her skin. Taking care of your mind is important too. Meditation and yoga are ways to care for your body and mind at the same time. Additionally, eating healthy foods and getting enough sleep can boost your mood and make you feel your best.

CHAPTER FOUR

HOW DO I LOOK?

In 2018, one in ten girls in the United States had an eating disorder. The most common disorders were anorexia and bulimia. Many girls obsessed over food or had a distorted view of their bodies.

Girls with anorexia see themselves as fat even if they are at a healthy weight or underweight. They often avoid eating or diet until they become extremely thin for their body type. Girls with bulimia may stay at a normal body weight, but they have unhealthy eating habits. They eat large amounts of food at one time and then make themselves vomit. This behavior is also known as binging and purging.

Other people may struggle with disordered eating. A girl who struggles with disordered eating has an unhealthy relationship with food or her body, but her situation isn't as severe as a diagnosed eating disorder.

Eating disorders are complicated illnesses. Researchers can't yet fully explain what causes them, but they have identified

Girls who suffer from eating disorders are not alone, and eating disorders affect people of all ages.

several risk factors. Often a combination of factors leads to an eating disorder, including genetics, life events, and media or peer pressure. Certain habits such as dieting have also shown to increase a person's risk of developing an eating disorder. Girls who suffer from eating disorders are not alone, and eating disorders affect people of all ages. Still, many girls hide their symptoms from loved ones.

DESTINY'S STORY

Destiny sat at the island in her kitchen. She scrolled down her social media feed, looking at posts from her favorite celebrities. *They're all so skinny. I could never look like that*, Destiny thought. She closed the app and went to the fridge to find a snack. She ended up eating a handful of chips and an ice cream sandwich, and soon it was time for dinner. Her friend Penny was picking her up to go out.

"Hey, Destiny!" Penny said, as Destiny opened the car door. "How are ya?"

TALK ABOUT IT

- **Do you often see images of thin models? How often? What kind of message do you think those images send? How do they make you feel?**
- **When others compliment your looks, how does it make you feel?**
- **In your opinion, what types of compliments are the best? Why?**

"Good," Destiny said. "You?"

"Great! Wow, that shirt looks good on you. Where did you get it?" Penny asked.

"Thanks. And I don't remember. I've had it for a while," Destiny responded, as she tugged it down. She thought it felt a little tight.

***

Destiny couldn't decide what to order for dinner. She felt guilty for eating those treats earlier and wanted to get something small. At the same time, some of the pictures on the menu looked delicious.

"Do you know what you're going to get?" Penny asked.

"I can't decide . . ."

"Me either! The dinner special sounds so good, but I know it will be a ton of food!" Penny chatted about a few other dinner options while Destiny debated her options in her head.

I could just get an appetizer or a side dish. That would make up for all the snacks I ate. But what if Penny asks me why I'm not eating a meal? I should get the special. After all, Penny doesn't know I spoiled my dinner with snacks.

"I think I'm going to get pasta," Penny finally stated. "Have you decided?" She looked at Destiny and smiled.

"Yeah, I'm going to get the special," Destiny said. She smiled back at her friend.

***

I can't believe I ate all that, Destiny thought.

Destiny took another bite. She was already full, but the food was delicious. She pushed her guilt about the snacks out her mind.

Eventually, the leftover mess on Destiny's plate began to gross her out. She placed her napkin over it, but the large, dirty plate was still right under her nose. *I can't believe I ate all that*, Destiny thought.

Destiny went to the bathroom before they left. Her stomach was so full that she felt like it could burst. She wished she hadn't eaten so much. Destiny made herself vomit and then washed her face quickly at the sink. "I'm never going to do that again," she said to herself. But she knew it wasn't true. She had made that promise before.

"Are you all right?" Penny asked when Destiny got back to the table. "You were in the bathroom for a bit," she said.

"Oh, yeah, I'm fine," Destiny said.

"Okay," Penny said.

TALK ABOUT IT

- **Have you ever felt guilty for eating? What did you do to make yourself feel better?**
- **Destiny struggled to make a decision about her food. What reason or motivation did she have for ordering a small dinner? What about the larger dinner? Do you think those reasons are healthy? Why or why not?**

Destiny looked at her feet as they walked to the car. She knew Penny was looking at her. Last week, Penny had caught Destiny throwing up in the bathroom. Destiny had the water running to try to drown out the noise, but she thought Penny still heard. Penny didn't say anything at the time, but now Destiny felt awkward.

"Destiny, I'm worried about you," Penny said while they drove home. "My cousin used to do the same thing, but then she started seeing a therapist."

"Okay," Destiny said. She hoped Penny would drop the subject.

"Why don't you just stop?" Penny asked quietly. They both knew Penny was talking about Destiny binging and purging.

Destiny looked out the window. Tears were forming in her eyes. She was frustrated. Penny made it sound like that was an easy decision. She didn't respond.

"Destiny? I'm sorry, I don't know how to help—" Penny started.

"I feel like you're judging me!" Destiny interrupted her. She didn't mean to lash out at her friend. At that moment, they arrived at Destiny's house. "Um, thanks for driving. I'll see you later."

"Bye," Penny said. Destiny jumped out of the car and fled inside as fast as she could.

Destiny crawled onto her bed. She texted Penny and apologized for her outburst. Then she thought about what Penny said. Maybe it was time to face the problem. *I think I have an eating disorder,* Destiny thought. That was the first time she admitted it to herself. Destiny knew she needed professional help, but she wanted to go one step at a time. First, she decided to be honest with Penny. Maybe Penny could help her figure out what to do.

TALK ABOUT IT

- **What would you do if you were Penny and suspected Destiny had an eating disorder? Would you do the same thing? Why or why not?**
- **Who else could Destiny go to for help?**

ASK THE EXPERT

Destiny's decision to be honest and ask for help was brave. Many people don't realize how their words can affect people with eating disorders. When Penny asked Destiny why she didn't just stop, she made Destiny feel ashamed of her behavior, as if she were choosing to have bulimia. One myth about eating disorders is that people choose them. But Destiny knew Penny cared about her and wanted to help. Even though Penny might have said the wrong things, Destiny hoped her friend could aid her in getting help.

Girls can help protect themselves and each other from developing an eating disorder by talking openly. Some ads, movies, and media messages show edited pictures of thin models. Discussing those messages helps everyone understand that the pictures are unrealistic and unhealthy examples. Body shapes vary, and there is no one definition of what is beautiful.

People don't choose eating disorders, but they can choose to get help. Doctors and therapists can help people recover mentally and physically. Treatment can be challenging. It may take months or years to recover from an eating disorder. But the ultimate goal is finding a healthy relationship with your body and food.

GET HEALTHY

- Watch for signs of an unhealthy diet. Behavior such as eating in secret, fearing certain foods, or avoiding activities or people can be a sign of an eating disorder.
- Surround yourself with supportive people. Positive experiences with family and friends can decrease your risk of developing an eating disorder.
- Focus on what you do and who you are, not what you look like. Healthy bodies come in all sizes.
- If you are struggling with an eating disorder or another unhealthy behavior, ask for help. Eating disorders, like other illnesses, require treatment to get better.

THE LAST WORD FROM EMMA

Conversations alone can't cause—or cure—an eating disorder. But you can help loved ones who are struggling by watching what you say. One idea is limiting how much you talk about food, clothes, or how you look. Many people who suffer from eating disorders think about those topics all the time. Saying you "feel fat" or that someone "looks great" can create stressful thoughts for someone with an eating disorder.

True friends are there for each other in good times and bad. If you or someone you love is struggling with an eating disorder, remember to reach out. Don't feel pressure to take on more than you know how to handle. Connect with an adult to get professional support. True friends who are honest and listen to each other can be a huge help on the path to healing.

CHAPTER FIVE

HIDDEN SUGAR

Sugar is in almost everything we eat—in places we expect, like ice cream and sweet treats, and even in places we don't, like salad dressing and bread. Some types of sugar are found naturally in foods, but many of the forms of sugar people consume daily aren't natural. They are made in labs and added to food and drink during processing. Added sugars include any sugar that is put into a food during its manufacture. They are common in processed foods. In fact, a 2016 US study found that 90 percent of the added sugars people ate came from processed foods.

Studies show that added sugar can cause serious health issues over time. For example, heart disease and type 2 diabetes can be caused at least in part by feeding the body too much sugar. The government's Dietary Guidelines for Americans recommend less than 10 percent of a person's diet is added sugars. For many people, 10 percent equals about 48 grams of sugar, which has about 200 calories. But sugar in foods and

To protect yourself from hidden sugar, it's important to be aware of how much and what types of sugar you consume.

drinks add up fast. On average, a 12-ounce (355 mL) can of soda has 160 calories, or 40 grams of sugar. A study from 2006 found sugary beverages such as soda, lemonade, sports drinks, and energy drinks were the largest source of added sugar for people in the United States.

Digesting lots of sugar takes a toll on a girl's organs. Her kidneys, liver, and brain are affected by sugar, and so are her teeth. Additionally, she is likely to gain weight from eating foods high in calories or sugar. Yet, sugar isn't bad for you in the right amounts and forms, such as the sugar found naturally in fruit. Breaking down sugar gives your body energy. To protect yourself from hidden sugar, it's important to be aware of how much and what types of sugar you consume.

JOY'S STORY

Naomi and Joy walked down a grocery store aisle. They looked for snacks to put in their lockers and backpacks. Naomi pushed the cart.

"Ooh, grab some granola bars for me," Naomi said.

Joy tossed some boxes in the cart. They landed on top of a package of fruit juice and a box of soda. Soda was Naomi's go-to drink, and juice was Joy's favorite. She drank some nearly every afternoon, along with a bag of chips or another snack.

Joy turned down the skin care aisle to get some face wash. She wanted to clear up her acne before the school dance in a few weeks. The girls then paid for their items and left. The next day, Joy reached for a snack and juice when her afternoon craving hit.

TALK ABOUT IT

- **When you choose a food or drink, do you think about whether it is healthy? Why or why not?**
- **Do you often have cravings between meals? Why do you think you get cravings? Is it because you're hungry from not eating enough food? Is it because you desire a certain flavor or food? Or is it another reason?**

***

On another trip, Joy walked down the aisle and scanned the shelves until she saw the logo she was looking for. It only took a few seconds before she recognized the label from commercials. When she was young, she did the activities on the back of the box. Now she played an online game based on the brand.

"I love this cereal," Joy said. "Have you ever had it?"

"Yeah, but my mom quit buying it a few years ago after her doctor told her she needed to eat less sugar," said Naomi, shrugging.

Joy looked at the box. The front label said *heart healthy*. Then Joy flipped the box. She read the nutrition facts and saw sugar was the second ingredient listed. She was shocked.

She read the nutrition facts and saw sugar was the second ingredient listed. She was shocked.

"Wow, I didn't realize how much sugar is in this," she said. *I thought cereal and milk were a healthy breakfast. Isn't that what most people eat?*

Joy frowned and put the box back on the shelf. Her feelings for the brand changed. She wanted to try new foods, especially ones with less sugar. Naomi's story reminded Joy of how eating too much sugar can lead to health issues.

TALK ABOUT IT

- **Do you have any favorite food or drink brands? Why are they your favorite?**
- **Do you often check the nutrition facts to see how much sugar is in a food or drink you're consuming? Why or why not?**

***

For the next few weeks, Joy tried different cereals after checking the nutrition labels. She also ate oatmeal and berries a

few times. She drank water instead of fruit juice, adding lemon slices for flavor. Instead of snacking on sugary granola bars, she ate homemade granola.

Joy wasn't the only one who thought her new snacks were tasty. She often caught Naomi grabbing a handful of the crunchy granola from Joy's locker too. Before she knew it, Joy was seeing some benefits of eating better. Her acne cleared up in time for the school dance, and she had fewer cravings between meals.

ASK THE EXPERT

Joy originally got hunger cravings because she was eating food that lacked nutrients. The food and drink might have tasted good, but they didn't fill her with nutrients to fuel her body. Joy changed her diet with a few simple switches, and she cut out some unnecessary sugars. Eating whole foods made her body feel better.

Since the 1970s, the number of obese children and teens in the United States has tripled. In 2016, about 20 percent of US youth were obese. Around the world, 41 million children under the age of five were obese in 2016. Additionally, studies have shown that advertisements for unhealthy foods are targeted at youth and connected to the rise in childhood obesity.

Marketing schemes often connect emotions of happiness and fun to food in order to hook young people on certain food products. Many advertisements target youth through screens. Young people spend hours in front of screens daily. They take in images and messages from advertisements, and when they think about what to eat or buy, brands from the advertisements come to mind. Unfortunately, many of those foods are high in fat, sodium, and sugar.

One major way to keep track of hidden sugar is by checking labels. Many foods are processed with lots of added sugar. Even foods that taste savory, such as pasta sauce and salad dressing, tend to have sneaky added sugar.

GET HEALTHY

- Watch out for misleading advertisements. Sugar is commonly added to "low-fat" foods to take the place of the flavor lost when the fat is removed.
- Read the ingredients list and avoid foods with sugar in the top three ingredients. Sugar has many names, including cane sugar, corn syrup, fruit juice concentrate, molasses, fructose, and maltodextrin.
- Choose foods with minimal or no processing. Heavily processed foods are changed greatly from their natural state and have multiple or added ingredients.

THE LAST WORD FROM EMMA

When I was in high school, sugar was my weakness, and I often bought sweet snacks from the cafeteria. At those times, it was clear to me that I was eating sugar. What I didn't realize was the hidden sugar in other parts of my diet. Even when I focused on eating vegetables in a salad, the dressing was often full of sugar.

As I learned about hidden sugar from teachers and my doctor, I found ways to cut it out. But that doesn't mean I avoid sugar completely. I still eat sweet treats and drink lemonade made with sugar. The important difference is that now I'm more aware of the sugar I'm consuming, so I can enjoy each treat as a treat, instead of hiding it in my regular diet.

CHAPTER SIX

MAKING TIME FOR MOVING

M*e time* is often thought of as lying on a couch or eating a sweet treat. However, the true purpose of me time is keeping up with your health mentally and physically. Of course, relaxing and enjoying a treat from time to time can be refreshing. But moving is an important part of health too.

Exercising leads to low body fat, strong bones, and healthy habits that follow teens into adulthood. Studies have found that girls who exercise have better memories and academic performance. They also have longer attention spans. The Centers for Disease Control (CDC) recommends girls up to age 18 get 60 minutes of moderate-to-intense exercise each day. Moderate activity could be hiking or doing yard work. Intense activity

> One of the biggest challenges of exercise is making time for it.

includes running, jumping rope, or doing martial arts. At least three days per week, the activity should be vigorous. Vigorous activity means your heart is beating fast and you're breathing hard.

One of the biggest challenges of exercise is making time for it. But you can pick an activity that's right for you that also fits into your schedule. Not only does exercise keep your body healthy, but it can be a fun way to spend your time.

MAYA'S STORY

"Maya! Are you busy right now?" Maya's sister Vivi yelled.

"Yes, I've got homework!" Maya called back.

"Okay, never mind, then," she said.

"Busy," Maya said under her breath. "I don't even know where to start!"

Maya opened her backpack, and some papers fell out. She picked them up and put them in the recycling. The bin was full, so she took it out to the kitchen. A calendar hung on the door, and Maya saw a big red circle with the words *Vivi turns 12!* on it. Her sister's birthday was only three days away. Before Maya

knew it, 15 minutes had passed, and she still hadn't started her homework. She kept getting distracted.

"Ugh, I'm going for a walk," Maya said to Vivi when she passed her on the way to the door.

TALK ABOUT IT

- **Maya has lots to do, and she still decides to exercise. Do you think she is using her time wisely? Why or why not?**
- **What do you do when you're feeling stressed or anxious?**

Maya's mind was racing, and her heart was beating fast. She was under stress and felt like she had a million things to do. She had a history test in two days and needed to pack tennis shoes for gym class tomorrow. Her room was messy, and she wanted to make Vivi a nice birthday card.

With each step, Maya felt better. Her stress seeped away. She organized her to-do list in her mind as she walked. By the time she got home, she had a plan. She would study and then pack. Then she would make Vivi's card. If she had time, she would clean her room too.

With each step, Maya felt better. Her stress seeped away.

"How was your walk?" Vivi asked.

"Great," Maya replied. "I feel a lot better." She smiled to herself. *Maybe I should do that more often.*

TALK ABOUT IT

- **Is exercise a priority in your schedule? Why or why not?**
- **Besides exercising, how can you make time for yourself? What types of activities do you enjoy doing in your free time?**

Maya took more walks over the next few weeks. Then she started walking every day after school, even when she wasn't stressed. She just liked moving her body. She quickly noticed how much exercise helped her focus and feel better.

When the weather got cold, Maya didn't want to walk outside, but she missed her daily activity. Some days she struggled to focus on her homework.

TALK ABOUT IT

- **Where can you go in your community to be active?**
- **Have you ever taken an exercise class? If yes, what was it like and would you do it again? If not, what type of class would you want to try?**
- **Do you often try new activities? Why or why not? How can doing new things benefit someone?**
- **Do you often exercise alone or with others? What are some benefits of each situation?**

One day, Maya put on an extra jacket and biked around the neighborhood. She decided to stop at the community center for a drink at the water fountain. She forgot she had to bike uphill on the way there, and her legs were burning when she finally reached the top. Maya went inside and saw a poster on a bulletin board about a free yoga class. She checked the listed time. *I could come on Tuesday and try it out*, she thought. Maya smiled and biked back home.

Maya enjoyed her first yoga class. The instructor recommended some videos people could do at home, and on a rainy day a few weeks later, Maya tried it. Not only did she think yoga was fun, but she also felt more connected to herself than before. Yoga helped her move her body to improve her balance, strength, and flexibility, and it also connected her mind to the movements.

ASK THE EXPERT

Maya made exercising a priority because it helped her feel her best. When she was stressed or upset, moving her body helped take her mind off of what was bothering her. Additionally, she was proud of her accomplishments.

Many girls must work around tight schedules to fit in the right amount of exercise. Others lack safe, affordable, or convenient places to work out. However, many daily activities can add up. Some convenient physical activities are walking an extra lap at the store or stretching while watching TV. Doing chores or taking the stairs are other ways to be active without interrupting your day. Additionally, many free exercise resources are online.

Doing a variety of movements is good for your body. Stretching should be a part of all exercise activities, and it's also a great way to keep muscles from getting too tight or stiff. Strength exercises such as lifting weights or doing push-ups burns calories. They make your muscles and bones stronger and help you stay fit overall. Aerobic exercises such as walking, running, or swimming strengthen your heart and lungs. Each type of activity is important for creating a well-rounded routine.

GET HEALTHY

- Try exercising with others. Walking with a friend, doing an outdoor activity, or joining a team or club is an easy way to make exercise fun.
- Schedule exercise time to make it a habit. Some people write a time on their calendar. Others take multiple short walks at certain times of the day.
- Warm up before a workout and cool down afterward. It's important to prepare your body to avoid injury and to make time for recovery.
- Wear light, breathable clothes and comfortable shoes. Exercising in the right gear lets you move freely and safely.

THE LAST WORD FROM EMMA

Since I was in high school, I've scheduled my exercise time into the morning. At first, I tried running, but I didn't enjoy that activity as much as others. Yoga and high-intensity interval training (HIIT) were more fun for me. Yoga helped me be calm and focused on stressful days. HIIT workouts made me feel powerful and productive. Once I found exercise I liked, my routine was easier to follow.

Some days it is hard to get up when I hear my alarm, but I know it will be worth it. My body feels strong after exercising, and I start my day with a positive attitude. I feel good knowing I've accomplished a workout before breakfast. However, morning workouts aren't the best for everyone. Afternoons and evenings can be a great time to get active too!

CHAPTER SEVEN

THE FAD DIET

In 2018, 36 percent of US residents followed a regulated eating pattern of some type. Before and after photos can make losing weight look desirable and easy. Celebrities in ads encourage people to try fad diets. Media images of thin women emphasize the idea that thin is beautiful. Understandably, many girls are tempted to try fad diets. About half of all teen girls diet in an effort to change their bodies. However, more than 33 percent of those girls are already at a healthy weight.

Fad diets come and go. Dieters eat like prehistoric people, or count calories, or don't eat at all for periods of time. People take pills and do juice cleanses, consuming little but juice for days. One fad diet focuses on eating healthy fats and limiting carbohydrates. The theory is that the body burns fat for fuel instead of getting energy from breaking down carbohydrates. Doctors advise some people with diabetes to follow this diet to help manage the disease. They also prescribe it to some children with seizures. Following this diet can lead to the desired results

Finding how to balance your body's nutrition is a very personal process.

for some people, but it is often used to lose weight rather than achieve health benefits.

It might sound easy to follow a prewritten diet plan, but every person's body is unique and needs different amounts of food and nutrients. Finding how to balance your body's nutrition is a very personal process.

HAILEY'S STORY

Hailey set her lunchbox down on the gray table in the cafeteria. She sat next to her friends. They packed lunches because they were doing a fad diet together. They didn't eat grains such as wheat or oats. They also avoided salt, dairy products, and potatoes. The diet focused on lean meats and green vegetables. It wasn't easy, but the girls agreed that it was a healthy way to eat. Several of their favorite celebrities swore by the diet, although none of the girls had talked to her doctor about it.

"Hi, Hailey!" Lauren said.

"Hey, Lauren, what did you bring for lunch today?"

"Broiled salmon, asparagus, and cauliflower rice. What about you?" Lauren asked, poking her fork into the peach-colored fish in her lunchbox.

"Yum! I've got a salad with chicken, cucumbers, and walnuts," Hailey responded. "Oh, I forgot a fork. I'll be right back."

Hailey walked across the tiled floor. She grabbed a napkin and fork from a counter. She saw packaged snacks and chips for sale. She turned her back on the treats. People walked past with trays holding pasta and a bread roll. *Mmmm,* Hailey thought, *a warm, buttered roll sounds delicious.* Then a friend waved at her from across the room. Hailey waved back and returned to her seat, pushing the forbidden roll out of her mind.

***

TALK ABOUT IT

- What diets or eating patterns do you know about? Would you consider following one? Why or why not?
- Have you and a friend or group of friends ever made a diet, exercise, or lifestyle decision together? If so, what was it? If not, how do you think making a pact helps people stick to their decisions?

A few days later, Hailey helped her mom unload the groceries.

"I got you these vitamins," her mom said, "since you aren't eating certain foods. I just

wish I knew more about your diet so I could make sure you're staying healthy."

"Thanks," Hailey replied. "And for the record, I've been feeling great lately."

When Hailey first started the fad diet, she felt really tired. Her body had to adjust to a new energy source. After several days, Hailey noticed her weight start to drop and her energy levels pick up again. She was pleased because she hoped this diet could help her lose some weight.

TALK ABOUT IT

- **What questions about eating habits or certain types of food do you have for a doctor or health professional?**
- **What are some reasons to limit eating grains?**
- **Do you think it is dangerous to follow a fad diet? Why or why not?**

Hailey closed the refrigerator door. Her mom turned and stacked some cans in the cupboard.

"Your fad diet may be popular, but I don't think it's healthy in the long run," she said.

"Why not?" Hailey asked.

"Well, a balanced diet doesn't leave out food groups.

"Your fad diet may be popular, but I don't think it's healthy in the long run."

And certain types of fat can build up and lead to heart problems," her mom replied.

"Hmm, I haven't thought about long-term effects," Hailey admitted. She sat at the kitchen table, and her mother sat down next to her.

TALK ABOUT IT

- **What food groups make up the most of your meals?**
- **Are there any food groups you have forgotten about or should eat more often?**
- **How might you change your everyday eating to ensure it is balanced?**

"Food groups are a great place to start when determining what to eat to fuel your body," said Hailey's mom. Hailey leaned back into the chair and listened. Her mom continued, "Think through each group: lean meat, whole grains, dairy, vegetables, fruits, and healthy fats. Decide which groups you may not be getting enough of and which ones you may be eating too much. Variety is the other key to a healthy eating." She smiled at Hailey.

Hailey felt like a lightbulb went on in her head. Eating healthy didn't require eliminating foods. She smiled back at her mom and decided to talk to her friends about ending their diet.

ASK THE EXPERT

Hailey and her friends wanted to eat healthy and lose weight, so they started a fad diet. However, they didn't consult with their doctors first and therefore could be putting themselves at risk for health issues. The diet might not be giving their bodies some essential nutrients. Then Hailey's mom reminded her that balanced diets offer more ways to get the right nutrients. Variety and portions are the key to eating healthy.

Fad diets offer results that seem too good to be true. Girls may think there is no harm in trying a diet, but many diets aren't sustainable. In other words, they are hard to continue for reasons such as food type, habit, or cost. For example, the paleo diet depends on meat, which can be very expensive. And many such diets are unhealthy in the long run.

The real solution to making healthy lifestyle changes is education. Girls who learn about balanced diets can make smarter choices in grocery stores and school cafeterias. If they know which foods are full of nutrients, they can eat healthy meals for the rest of their lives. And many girls won't need to follow a diet. Doctors and dieticians can help you create a food and exercise plan that works for you. After all, everyone's body, budget, and lifestyle are unique.

GET HEALTHY

- Aim to learn about nutrients your body needs before following an eating pattern. Many fad diets aren't sustainable.
- Don't eliminate food groups. Focus on variety and amount of each type of food.
- Balance your meal by making half the plate fruits and vegetables and half grains, dairy, and protein. Mix up protein from meal to meal by eating seafood, beans, eggs, meat, and poultry.
- Talk to your doctor or a nutritionist if you want advice or assistance in figuring out what is healthy for you.

THE LAST WORD FROM EMMA

I find learning about my body interesting and empowering. I like knowing what foods make me feel my best and give me the right nutrients. For example, I know that eating grains or starches will give me energy. I know that protein helps me build muscle, recover, and get stronger after working out.

Fad diets are less tempting to me because I know what my body needs. A healthy meal for me has multiple parts and often multiple colors! Fruits and vegetables brighten up my plate. I focus on eating all the food groups throughout the week, which makes eating fun. I can enjoy all kinds of foods instead of trying to avoid certain food groups.

CHAPTER EIGHT

GOT CAFFEINE?

Caffeinated beverages are a part of daily life for many girls. Some drink soda with their lunch or as an afternoon treat. Others go to coffee shops with friends or to do homework. Some girls brew coffee at home in the morning and drink a cup before school.

One reason why caffeine is a part of many people's lives is because it is so easy to get. Many restaurants offer coffee, especially during breakfast hours. Coffee shops add flavors and creams to fit nearly any preference. Vending machines and gas stations sell a wide variety of soda and energy drinks. Dozens of flavors and bright labels make them look fun to drink too.

Caffeine may be cheap and easy to get, but it is still a drug. It is made naturally by some plants, and it can also be made artificially and added to food or drink. Like other drugs, it has side effects, especially if someone has too much. Many people value its positive side effects more than the negative ones. But teens who drink caffeine should think about how much they are having and why.

DEENA'S STORY

"Cappuccino for Deena?" called the barista from behind a counter. Deena stepped out of line in the crowded café to grab her drink. She saw the steam rising out of the small hole in the lid. When the scent of coffee reached her nose, she breathed deeply and smiled. Deena left the café and headed home.

The cool fall weather convinced her stop at the café for coffee rather than buy soda from the school vending machine. She had started drinking a caffeinated beverage every day after school in order to have enough energy and focus to do her homework. Before she started drinking coffee or soda after school, Deena usually walked directly to the couch. She would watch TV and rest because she was drained from a full day in classes.

When Deena got home, she took her backpack to her room. She unloaded her gym clothes and put her phone on the charger. Then she brought

TALK ABOUT IT

- **Do you have a routine before or after school? Does it involve any certain foods or drinks?**
- **Do you drink caffeine regularly? If yes, what do you drink and how often do you have it?**
- **Is there a time of day that you are often tired? Why do you think you get tired then? If not, can you imagine how and why Deena often gets tired after school?**

a textbook and notebook downstairs to the kitchen table. She planned to take notes for a quiz she had the next day.

By the time Deena was done taking notes, it was time for dinner. She felt relieved that she finished her work, and she was excited to have free time that night. On nights when she didn't get her homework done before dinner, she tended to feel stressed.

When Deena had free time after dinner, she often watched a movie or spent time with a friend. Deena decided to call Alison, who lived nearby.

"Hey, Deena!" Alison answered the phone.

"Alison! Wanna hang out tonight? I could walk to your place in a few minutes," Deena said.

"Actually, I've got too much homework right now," Alison responded. "But holiday break starts this weekend, so we can definitely get together then!"

"Okay," Deena said, "sounds good to me! I'll see you at school. Bye."

"Yeah, bye!" Alison said, before they hung up.

Deena ended up watching two movies that night. She knew the second movie wouldn't be done until after midnight, but she really wanted to see it. She didn't care if she got less sleep.

***

On the first day of holiday break, Deena stayed in her pajamas and enjoyed having so much time to herself. She went to bed at her normal time. The next day, she woke up without an alarm without any trouble. Deena continued to get more sleep than usual over break because she loved feeling rested.

TALK ABOUT IT

- **How do you manage your time when you have work to do?**
- **What do you do when you have free time during the week? How does having free time make you feel?**
- **How might you change your habits so you can get more sleep?**

She didn't remember her caffeine routine until she went back to school.

For several days, Deena didn't have caffeine. She noticed a slight headache the first two days, but once she was distracted by Alison or another activity, she forgot about it. Eventually, she wrote the paper she was assigned for holiday break without needing caffeine to focus. She didn't remember her caffeine routine until she went back to school. *Oh yeah,* she thought, *I haven't had soda for more than a week! I'll pick some up this afternoon on my way home. I'll probably need it since I've got a test coming up on Friday.*

Deena drank the soda quickly after school. It tasted great, but it didn't make her feel as good as usual. Her stomach was upset from the sugar and carbonation. She was a little jittery from the caffeine too. She kept tearing small bits of paper off her notebook and folding them into tiny balls. Then, she would shake her head at the mess she created, sweep the pile of balls into her hand, and get up to throw them away. After doing this twice, Deena was frustrated. *Why was it so hard to focus?*

That night, Deena had a slight headache, which made finishing her homework even harder. As soon as she completed it, she went to bed early. Luckily, she felt better the next day. She decided to skip the afternoon soda. To her surprise, she had no

trouble doing her homework. She took notes for a class and completed two worksheets.

Deena thought about how her routine before and after break had changed. Then she decided to stop getting coffee or soda after school. She planned to get enough sleep to be alert instead. Additionally, she looked forward to having more money for other things.

TALK ABOUT IT

- **Do you feel like you get enough sleep? If yes, where did you learn your healthy sleeping habits? If not, why don't you get enough?**
- **Do you depend on caffeine to do certain things? If yes, do you think you truly need it? Have you ever tried changing your routine? Why or why not?**
- **Do you think drinking caffeine regularly is a healthy habit? Why or why not?**

ASK THE

EXPERT

Caffeine is known for positive side effects such as enhanced mood, energy, and alertness. However, it can affect teens differently than adults. It can slow brain development or make it hard to fall asleep. It can also cause headaches, upset stomachs, and increased heart rates. These negative side effects can be worse for young people or people who are sensitive to caffeine.

The American Academy of Pediatrics recommends teens have no more than 100 mg of caffeine per day. That's about the amount of caffeine in one can of soda or a home-brewed cup of coffee, but most energy drinks and drinks from coffee shops have more caffeine than that. Limiting caffeine to that amount can protect you from experiencing negative side effects or becoming dependent on caffeine. Caffeine dependency occurs when someone needs caffeine to get through the day and has trouble cutting back on how much he or she drinks. Caffeine dependency can happen before people know it. In fact, 75 percent of children and overall 80 percent of people worldwide have caffeine every day.

In addition to caffeine, many sodas have lots of sugar, up to 50 grams per 12-ounce (355 mL) can. Sugar and caffeine combined can produce stronger side effects. For these reasons, you should be aware of how much caffeine you put in your body.

GET HEALTHY

- Beware of energy drinks. Many have dangerously high doses of caffeine, up to 500 mg or the amount of caffeine in 14 cans of soda.
- Fill your backpack, refrigerator, or glass with caffeine-free drinks such as milk or water. Make healthy drinks part of your daily diet, and cut out caffeinated drinks or limit them as a special treat.
- Read nutrition labels and check the amount of caffeine in the drink you want to buy.
- Pay attention to your body and how you feel. You might experience negative side effects of caffeine but not realize the cause. Once you identify what you're feeling, you can take action to cut back or eliminate what's causing the issues.

THE LAST WORD FROM EMMA

In high school, many of my friends drank even more caffeinated beverages than usual while studying. One friend often joked that she needed caffeine to make it through each day, but I worried about her when she was stressed or not getting enough sleep. She turned to caffeine for boosts of energy and focus instead of listening to her body.

Since I didn't like the carbonation in soda and I thought coffee tasted really bitter, I didn't bother with caffeinated drinks. My friends teased me and told me I was crazy! They didn't know how I woke up early or stayed focused to prepare for big tests. Sometimes I felt left out, but I know caffeine isn't for everyone. You need to decide for yourself what foods and drinks make you feel the best.

5
6

CHAPTER NINE

TRAINING FOR TRYOUTS

Training and setting goals to improve your physical performance can be a great way to create healthy habits. Working toward a goal can increase confidence, improve fitness, and help athletes recover from sports injuries.

If *training* sounds too formal or structured, just think about different ways of moving your body. What types of exercises interest you, and how can you get better at them? Not only can exercise make you feel proud of yourself and your body, but it also helps your brain, muscles, bones, and entire body stay healthy. Additionally, working toward a goal and reaching it can be really rewarding. If you're active in a sport, challenging yourself to be better is a great way to see success in your next competition.

BETH'S STORY

The marker squeaked as Beth drew another black X on the calendar. She was one day closer to soccer tryouts. She wanted to be a starting player this year, so she created a fitness routine to help herself improve. She wrote her big and small goals in a journal. A few times a week, she took time to write in the journal about her progress and how she felt.

Beth's biggest goal was to be a starting midfielder. Players in that position do the most running, and they are often a big part of the action in a game. Midfielders help on defense and get to run toward the goal during offensive plays. One of Beth's other goals was to run at least 6 miles (9.7 km) a week. She wanted to build her endurance so she wouldn't get as winded during games.

Some of Beth's small goals included being a supportive teammate and improving her footwork.

***

"Nice kick, Beth!" Padma yelled. Beth and Padma were playing soccer together.

"Thanks!" Beth responded. "I've been working on my corner kicks all week."

TALK ABOUT IT

- **Do you have any fitness goals right now? If yes, what are they? If not, what is one fitness goal you would be interested in setting?**
- **Reflect on the past several weeks, months, or years. Has your fitness routine changed at different times of the year? What is it like right now?**

She smiled and chased the soccer ball. *It feels good when someone sees my hard work paying off*, Beth thought. She dribbled the ball back to where her teammate stood. The next second, Padma rolled the ball under her foot and spun her body while taking a step forward.

"Nice move," Beth complimented her, still playing over what she just saw in her head. "Can you teach me that?"

"Sure!" Padma replied.

For the next few minutes, Beth and Padma worked side by side. Beth learned the move quickly. It wasn't as hard as it looked.

The girls paused to get a drink of water. Then they stepped back on the field, passing and shooting more goals. Before Beth knew it, her stomach was rumbling. She checked her phone and saw it was almost dinner time.

"I've got to get home for dinner," Beth told Padma as she packed her ball in her bag.

"Oh, yeah, me too," Padma said. "Want to practice again tomorrow?"

"I was thinking of lifting weights," Beth said. "If I get a bit stronger, I'll be able to send the ball farther downfield. Anyway, you're welcome to join me."

"Good idea! I will," Padma said.

Day by day, Beth worked at her strength and skills. She stuck to her healthy routine. Beth did something active each weekday and rested on weekends. A few times each week, she practiced with Padma and other teammates. Some days she worked out on her own. Beth noticed her legs and lungs feeling stronger. During scrimmages, she was the last one to get tired, and she often outran other girls to the ball.

TALK ABOUT IT

- **When you are working toward a goal, do you tend to tell others about it or keep it to yourself? Have you ever tried doing the opposite?**
- **What challenges do you think Beth faced while focusing on her training routine?**
- **How would you overcome physical or mental challenges if you changed your routine? How would you motivate yourself to stay on track?**

"Good luck tomorrow!" Beth called to a few teammates after a practice session.

"You too!" one replied, waving back.

"Yeah, see you tomorrow at tryouts!" Padma said.

Beth woke up with a smile on her face. It was tryout day. She had worked hard, and now she could show her coaches how much she had improved. Beth pulled on her clothes and checked that her soccer bag was packed. Then she walked downstairs for breakfast. She was a bit nervous but mostly excited.

Beth woke up with a smile on her face.

School seemed to last longer than usual. In the hallways, Beth noticed other girls looking nervous. She gave them a thumbs-up. Finally, the bell rang.

Beth changed clothes and walked out to the soccer field. She smiled when she saw her teammates and coaches. She couldn't wait to try out.

TALK ABOUT IT

- **Do you think Beth will continue her routine? Or will she check off each goal she completed and be done with it? What would you do?**
- **How did changing her exercise routine help Beth prepare for tryouts, both physically and mentally?**
- **In what ways could you change your routine to improve your health?**

ASK THE EXPERT

Beth knew how she wanted to improve and why. Some of her goals were things she could measure, such as running a certain amount each week. Others were just about making progress or getting better. In the end, she walked into soccer tryouts feeling confident and proud. She had worked hard on her skills, strength, and endurance. No matter what position she earned on the team, she knew she was a better player than she had been before. What she may not have realized is that her exercise routine also gave her a healthy mind-set. She felt happy and confident and spread her positive feelings to others.

If you are trying to improve your physical performance, try focusing on one day at a time. The most important part of training is progress. No one is perfect, and if you try to be perfect, you may end up more stressed than when you started. Be sure to include recovery days in your routine. Be flexible when schedules change or weather gets in the way. Life can be difficult from time to time, but don't let it stop you from reaching your goals.

GET **HEALTHY**

- Write down or talk to others about your goals. Goals and support from others can help you stay motivated.
- Create a routine and stick to it. Routines quickly become a new normal, and they don't have to be exactly the same each day.
- Challenge yourself with a new skill or activity. You might be surprised at what you can learn or what natural talents you didn't know you had.
- Set a deadline or train for a specific event. Having a limited time period to improve performance helps many people stay focused.
- Practice proper form. Take time to learn the right ways to stretch, lift weights, or do any other new movement. Learning the right way to do certain exercises shows responsibility and makes exercising safer.

THE LAST WORD FROM **EMMA**

I played many sports growing up and continued dance and track in high school. Unfortunately, I suffered minor injuries over the years and found myself feeling nervous about testing my body. I was scared to fail. I also didn't want others to see me struggling with different activities. But I knew that the best way to get back my skills—and to get rid of those negative thoughts—was to train. What helped me improve my physical activity was creating small goals and sticking to my routine. Doing one more push-up than the week before showed me progress. Racing a teammate encouraged us both to be better. I focused on myself instead of looking for approval from others. Eventually, when I reached my goals, I felt excited to set and work toward new ones.

A SECOND LOOK

Throughout this book, we have seen a girl struggle with an eating disorder and another who learned about reading food labels. We saw a girl who followed a diet and another who trained and reached her fitness goal.

You might relate to some of these stories. Others may have surprised you or got you thinking in a new way. But one thing is sure: a girl's health is directly affected by her diet and exercise. When she chooses healthy habits, she may see results in a few days. Her mood might change, or her skin might seem clearer. Or she may see results over her lifetime. She may develop a positive body image or regular exercise routine. Not only does your body benefit from healthy food and fitness, but those habits help your mind too.

In the end, you only have one body. It's your job to take care of it and use it to make a difference in the world. Let healthy nutrition and exercise habits be part of your life. Journaling about your feelings, your talents, and your interests can help you create a healthy exercise plan. You can prioritize workouts and rest days. You can challenge yourself solo or enjoy activities with friends. As for eating healthy, small changes can make a big difference. Limiting certain ingredients such as sugar and caffeine can protect your body from future health problems. Focusing on eating from all the food groups can lead you to try new flavors, and journaling your meals can help keep you on track.

No magic diet or perfect exercise routine exists. Everyone is unique, and you must decide for yourself what makes you feel your best.

PAY IT FORWARD

Nutrition and exercise are all about finding the right balance. Discovering what makes you feel your best is a journey that changes throughout your life. Now that you know what to focus on, you can pay it forward to a friend too. Remember the Get Healthy tips throughout this book, then take these steps to get healthy and get going.

1. **Work with your family to create grocery lists and meal plans so that cooking at home is easier. Following a list can help you avoid spending money on fast food and processed foods, which are often unhealthy and more expensive than simpler, natural foods.**

2. **Read labels on the back of food and drink products to find items with short ingredient lists and no added sugar. If you find hidden sugar or high amounts of caffeine in something, you may not want to consume it regularly.**

3. **Write down a few activities you enjoy doing and check your schedule to see how exercise fits in it. If you have time, invite a friend to exercise with you, or set a goal to challenge yourself by training or learning a new skill.**

4. Listen to your body and remember to rest after exercising so you don't become exhausted.

5. Eating disorders can be caused by many things, such as negative body image, poor diet, or unhealthy exercise habits. To lower your risk of developing an eating disorder, talk openly with supportive family and friends.

6. Talk with your doctor before making a big change in your nutrition or exercise routine, such as following a fad diet or doing rigorous physical activities.

7. Focus on eating a variety of foods instead of eliminating food groups. Eating the right portions of food can help your body feel its best.

8. Give meaningful compliments to friends that aren't about their bodies or their looks. Encouraging others' personalities, skills, or hard work is a great way to show them you care.

GLOSSARY

allergic
Having a strong, abnormal immune response to something.

antioxidant
A substance in food that prevents harmful chemical reactions involving oxygen.

artificially
By humans rather than naturally.

broiled
Cooked directly under heat.

calorie
A unit to measure how much energy or heat a food or drink can produce when consumed.

compulsive
Having powerful urges to do something.

diabetes
A disease in which a person's body doesn't properly process sugar.

distorted
Altered or changed from the truth or a normal state.

endurance
The ability to continue doing a stressful activity.

genetics
The combination of traits that parents pass on to their children.

industry
The overall people, money, and businesses in a certain type of work.

obese
Having a much higher amount of body fat than what would be healthy for a person's body.

pact
A group agreement.

processed
Food that has been cooked, packaged, frozen, or changed.

scrimmage
A competition played as practice.

sodium
An element combined with chloride to make salt.

ADDITIONAL

RESOURCES

SELECTED BIBLIOGRAPHY

"Eating Disorders in Teens." *American Academy of Child & Adolescent Psychiatry*, Mar. 2018, aacap.org.

"Facts about Saturated Fats." *MedlinePlus*, 6 Nov. 2019, medlineplus.gov.

"Fitting in Fitness: Finding Time for Physical Activity." *Mayo Clinic*, 27 Sept. 2019, mayoclinic.org.

FURTHER READINGS

Castle, Jill. *Eat Like a Champion*. American Management Association, 2015.

Foran, Racquel. *Living with Eating Disorders*. Abdo, 2014.

Maring, Therese Kauchak. *Sports & Fitness: How to Use Your Body and Mind to Play and Feel Your Best*. American Girl, 2018.

ONLINE RESOURCES

To learn more about nutrition and exercise, please visit **abdobooklinks.com** or scan this QR code. These links are routinely monitored and updated to provide the most current information available.

MORE INFORMATION

For more information on this subject, contact or visit the following organizations:

National Eating Disorders Association (NEDA)

1500 Broadway, Suite 1101
New York, NY 10036
nationaleatingdisorders.org
1-800-931-2237

NEDA supports individuals and families affected by eating disorders throughout the United States. The organization funds research, connects people in communities, and raises awareness about eating disorders.

President's Council on Sports, Fitness, and Nutrition (PCSFN)

1101 Wootton Parkway, Suite 420
Rockville, MD 20852
hhs.gov/fitness/index.html
1-240-276-9567

The PCSFN promotes active healthy lifestyles for all US citizens. It shares blog articles and research results, as well as supporting sports and activities around the country.

United States Food and Drug Administration (FDA)

10903 New Hampshire Ave.
Silver Spring, MD 20993-0002
fda.gov/home
1-888-436-6332

The FDA reviews food products in the United States and requires companies to follow certain guidelines and labels.

INDEX

acne, 57, 59
addiction, 29, 39
adrenaline, 38
advertisement, 9, 13, 17, 20, 26, 60–61
alarm clock, 30
all natural, 19, 23–24
American Academy of Pediatrics, 90
antioxidant, 19
anxiety, 29, 66
athlete, 93

bacon, 16
balanced diet, 77, 80
binging, 41, 46–48
body image, 29, 38
bone loss, 29
brand, 23, 57–58, 60
budget, 19, 80
burger, 12
buzzwords, 26

caffeine, 83–84, 88–91
calories, 9, 16, 53–54, 70, 73
candy, 23–24
carbohydrates, 73
Centers for Disease Control (CDC), 63
cereal, 23, 57–58
chips, 19, 23, 42, 57, 75
coffee shop, 83, 90
cortisol, 38
coworker, 12
craving, 57, 59–60

diabetes, 9, 17, 53, 73
Dietary Guidelines for Americans, 53
drive-through, 9

eating disorders, 29, 41–42, 46–48, 50–51
    anorexia, 41
    bulimia, 41, 46–48, 50
energy drinks, 54, 83, 90–91
exercise, 6–7, 16, 29–39, 63–64, 66–68, 70–71, 76, 80, 93, 98, 100
exhaustion, 38

fad diet, 73–74, 77–78, 80–81
fast food, 6, 9–10, 12–17
fruit, 17, 54, 78, 81

genetics, 42
gluten free, 20, 22–23, 25
goals, 27, 50, 93–94, 97–98, 100–101
granola bar, 20, 22, 57, 59
grocery store, 10, 15–16, 54, 80
gym, 29–30, 34, 66

habit, 6–7, 10, 13, 15–16, 34, 41–42, 63, 71, 77, 80, 87, 89, 93
headache, 34, 88, 90
heart disease, 9, 17, 53
high-intensity interval training (HIIT), 71
homework, 37, 64, 66–67, 83–84, 86–89
hormones, 38

ice cream, 42, 53
immune system, 38
internet, 24

label, 19, 23–27, 57–58, 61, 83, 91
lifting weights, 30–31, 70, 97, 101
low fat, 26, 61

marketing, 19–20, 24, 26–27, 60
meditation, 39

National Center for Health Statistics, 16
newspaper, 24
nutrients, 9, 15, 39, 60, 74, 80–81

obese, 16, 60
organ, 54
organic, 20

packing a lunch, 10, 15, 17, 20, 74
peer pressure, 42
processed foods, 27, 53, 61
purging, 41, 46–48

restaurant, 9–10, 13, 17, 83
routine, 6, 29–30, 38–39, 70–71, 84, 88–89, 94, 97–98, 100–101
running, 6, 33, 64, 70–71, 94, 100

salad dressing, 53, 61
saturated fat, 9, 16–17
seizure, 73
self-conscious, 13
sleep, 34–35, 37–39, 87, 89–91
smoothie, 20
snacks, 15, 20, 42, 44, 46, 54, 57, 59, 61, 75
soccer, 94, 96, 98, 100
social media, 29, 42
soda, 19, 54, 57, 83–84, 88–91
sodium, 9, 20, 60
sore, 33, 39
strength, 37, 68, 70, 97, 100
stress, 30, 38, 51, 66–67, 70–71, 86, 91, 100
stretching, 33, 70, 101
sugar, 9, 16, 20, 23–24, 27, 53–54, 58–61, 88, 90
summer, 13–14
swimming, 33, 70

therapist, 38, 47, 50
trans fat, 16–17

underweight, 41
University of Houston, 26

vegetables, 20, 61, 74, 78, 81
vending machine, 83–84
vitamins, 76

weight, 9, 13–14, 16, 41, 54, 73–74, 77, 80
whole grain, 19–20, 23, 78

yoga, 39, 68, 71
YouTube, 12

ABOUT THE AUTHOR

EMMA HUDDLESTON

Emma Huddleston lives in Minnesota with her husband. She enjoys reading, writing, and swing dancing. She has three sisters and three brothers, and she is an aunt! She hopes this book reminds girls how strong they are and helps them create healthy habits as they grow into even stronger women.